SARA AND THE LONG LEGS

By: Ibrahim Ghorbandoost

Illustrator: Sahar Radhoosh

Sara and The Long Legs

Author: Ibrahim Ghorbandoost

Illustrator: Sahar Rahhoosh

Publisher: Supreme Century
Years of Publishing: 2020
ISBN : 9781939123978

With appreciation to my friends:

Dr. Mohammad Hossein Rezadoost,
Reza Abdolrezai
and
Dr. Shima Babapour.

In the Name of God, the Compassionate, the Merciful

Once upon a time, there was a lovely village among great mountains and forests. There were dwarf people living in this village. They had no friends outside their village since there was no other village nearby. The men only went out of the village every few days to get food in the forest.

The people in the village were terrified of the animals in the woods and felt safe while they were in the village because they thought that their village was surrounded by a halo of light that prevented strangers or animals from entering the village.

In this village, a little girl named Sara lived with her father. That day, Sara, like the friends of her age, was waiting for the next day festival, because they were going to celebrate for the girls who reached the age of nine. It was a tradition at the village that mothers gave a bracelet with sparkling stones to their daughters at the age of nine and from that date, they had to help their mothers besides playing. On the celebration day, the girls had to cook the festival meal with the help of adults.

But Sara did not remember her mother, Hilda.

Her father said that after her birth, her mother had left the village and never returned. Whenever she asked her father or the people of the village about her mother, she was not answered clearly, and everyone would tell a made-up story that misled Sara even more. She wanted to go after her mother, but she was always petrified to leave the village because there were always scary sounds coming from the woods. The adults said it was the sound of Long-Legs, the jungle monster. Anytime the Long-Legs' sound was heard, the country dwellers, particularly the kids, freaked out and so did Sara.

4

5

Day and night, the monster approached the village, whined, and screamed so loudly that the children hid under their blankets or rushed in fear to their parents because they thought the monster was going to eat them. An old man, named Goda, lived in the village and everyone in the village respected him.

Sara went to him on the feast day and asked Goda, "Why did my mother go to the forest, in spite of knowing the fact that it is a dangerous place?"

"Your mother was a very brave woman", Goda replied.

Sara asked, "Why didn't she return like everyone else?"

"That's the question you have to ask your father," Goda said. Sara hastily returned home and realized her father was not there. He, along with the other men of the village, had gone into the woods to prepare food for the celebration day. Sara was upset that her mother was not there to attend the celebration like everyone else. She thought to herself that she had asked about her mother from her father and the villagers but they had not answered her correctly so far, thus, she decided to look after her mother on her own. Sara gathered the necessary supplies and set off. She was very scared to leave the village for the first time but was sure that if she did not go, the fear would never let her go. So, she went from a way that the people of the village would not see her.

After walking for a while, Sara found herself in the woods. When she saw she was far from the village, fear engulfed her, but she remembered the old man said that Sara's mother was a courageous woman, so she went on.

In the woods, everything was beautiful like the village. The sparrows were accompanying Sara and it made her very joyful but she did not know which way to go, so she decided to go to a nearby hill to be able to see the village.

9

After a while, Sara was so far from the village that she could no longer see the village even from the top of the hill. It was getting dark. Sara wanted to go back and look for her mother the next day, but she could no longer go back to the village. She realized that she was lost in the woods.

It was very cold and Sara was starving. She ate some of the food she had brought with her, and in order to avoid the cold and darkness, she gathered some firewood and lit a fire with the matchbox she had brought from home and lay down by the fire. She was so tired that she fell asleep. In her dream, Sara saw her mother was going into the woods and she went after her, but suddenly she lost her among the trees and found herself in the middle of hungry wolves were going to fall upon her. As the wolf jumped on her, Sara woke up and found herself in the woods. The sound of the animals could be heard, but she was no longer afraid because she had a purpose and that was finding her mother.

Sara thought how to escape if an animal attacked her. It crossed her mind to carry a bright torch with her. She picked up a torch and waved it this way and that way to see her environment. She unexpectedly saw a large creature with big arms and long legs but its face resembled a man. The villagers called it Long-Legs. It was too big and Sara was too small and could not defend herself.

Sara started crying out of fear and called for her mother. The monster came to Sara and Sara, who could no longer resist, passed out. When Sara came round, she saw there was a cave at the top of the mountain and a fire was burning beside it.
As she got up to run away, the monster entered the cave. Sara silently stood still in fear.

Long-Legs approached her slowly and handed her a wild apple. Sara looked at Long-Legs inamazement. She thought the apple was poisonous and the monster noticed it, so it took the apple from her and began to eat it. She watched Long-Legs for a while and then stretched her hand. The monster smiled and gave another apple to Sara and they both started eating.

After a while, Sara asked, "Why do you scare the villagers?"

"I never wanted to frighten you. I am very lonely. Whenever I wanted to come to the villagers, they didn't allow me and were scared of me," the monster replied sadly.

Sara faced the monster in awe and asked, "Aren't you the cannibal monster?"

"No," the monster replied.

"Then, who are you?" Sara asked.

The next morning, when I woke up, I saw that I had grown up too much and I was scared as well and went straight to the village, and the villagers who had been searching for me in the woods ran away as they saw me and because they saw my own belongings in my hands, they thought I had eaten Tom Thumb and I was a cannibal monster. I did everything I could to tell them I was actually Tom Thumb. Only my mother recognized me. She came after me after giving birth to her second child. She was scared when she saw me at first, but after she recognized me, she stayed with me and did not return to the village again."

Wondered at Long-Legs' words, Sara thought for a moment, and asked, "Why didn't your mother come to the village and tell the villagers you are Tom Thumb?" It replied, "When I was tiny, everyone made fun of me and my mother was upset and heart-broken. She knew that this time I would still be ridiculed for my tall height. She was angry with the people of the village; this is why she did not return."

Sara, who was now totally relaxed, asked, "Why did you come near the village and scare the children with your voice?"

"I never wanted to scare anyone," Long-Legs replied, "Every time I came to the village, I felt sad by seeing the children and the villagers and began to cry and whine."

Now, the sky had brightened up and Long-Legs and Sara had established an amicable relationship.

Long-Legs told Sara, "Now, it's time to go back. I bet everybody is looking for you."

"I am looking for my mother and I have to find her," Sara said.

Long-Legs said, "Maybe my mother knows her."

16

The monster said, "I was from your village too. When I was born, I was unlike other kids. I was too tiny, so everyone called me Tom Thumb and I was always upset about why I had to stay that way until the end of my life. Lastly, I went to the village of sage. I asked him to tell me the secret of height growth, and Goda said, "All that God has given is good", but I insisted. Goda said, "The stories say there is a spring at the Silan Mountain peak in a cave and you have to go there. After reaching there, drink only one sip of water from that fountain and afterward, you will also grow up to the same height as the village people."

Therefore, I set off without my parents' permission. The mountain road was far away. All the water I had taken along was finished in the middle of the road. When I reached the spring, I was so tired that I forgot I was only allowed to drink one sip of water and thus, I drank to my heart's content and fell asleep right there due to fatigue.

Sara was happy and asked Long-Legs to go to its mother. They set out in the woods. On the way, Sara thought about Long-Legs' life story and a question came to her mind and asked, "What is your mother's name, Long-Legs?"

"Hilda," Long-Legs replied.

So, Sara walked faster. She was just thinking on the way and her enthusiasm had increased much more. They reached a hut in the middle of the forest by a pond. A beautiful woman was washing clothes by the pond. As the woman noticed Long-Legs and Sara, she got up and looked at them in surprise.

Sara went forward and said, "I come from the White Village, my name is Sara and my father's name is Yata. I am looking for my mother whom I have lost after my birth."

The woman did not say anything and her eyes were full of tears. She hugged Sara and said with a deep sigh, "My daughter Sara. Sara, I knew one day you would come to me."

Sara also began to cry and hugged her mother tightly. She was crying for joy this time. On the way, Sara had figured out that Long-Legs' mother was her own mother, and just a question had occupied her mind. When they entered the cabin, Sara asked her mother, "Why didn't the villagers tell me about my brother?"

"You had better ask them this question!" Hilda replied.

After a few days, Sara asked her mother and brother to go with her to the village. Hilda was reluctant to go back to the village but accepted due to Sara's persistence. However, Long-Legs wanted to go to the village as soon as possible.

They started to go and when they were near the village, the men who were outside the village ran away after seeing them and returned to the village. When Sara and Long Legs and her mother arrived at the village, everyone was silent upon seeing them.

Sara yelled, "Why didn't anyone tell me that my mother left the village to look for my brother? This is my mom, and that is the monster you are scared of."

Suddenly, people said, "We have to kill the monster," and attacked Long-Legs. Goda shouted abruptly, "Stop," and everyone stood still.

He went to the middle of the square and told them, "This monster is Tom Thumb who you used to mock and you still want to hurt him. I knew it was Tom Thumb but I knew too if I told you, you would not accept it."

Goda kept talking and said, "Don't you see that he penetrated the village's halo of light and came in?"

Everyone silently looked at each other in surprise. One of the residents asked, "How did Tom Thumb become a monster?"

21

They started to go and when they were near the village, the men who were outside the village ran away after seeing them and returned to the village. When Sara and Long Legs and her mother arrived at the village, everyone was silent upon seeing them.

Sara yelled, "Why didn't anyone tell me that my mother left the village to look for my brother? This is my mom, and that is the monster you are scared of."

Suddenly, people said, "We have to kill the monster," and attacked Long-Legs. Goda shouted abruptly, "Stop," and everyone stood still.

He went to the middle of the square and told them, "This monster is Tom Thumb who you used to mock and you still want to hurt him. I knew it was Tom Thumb but I knew too if I told you, you would not accept it."

Goda kept talking and said, "Don't you see that he penetrated the village's halo of light and came in?"

Everyone silently looked at each other in surprise. One of the residents asked, "How did Tom Thumb become a monster?"

To be continued...

www.ingramcontent.com/pod-product-compliance
Lightning Source LLC
Chambersburg PA
CBHW041009170626
46815CB00002B/230